TRIBES of NATIVE AMERICA

Arapaho

edited by Marla Felkins Ryan
and Linda Schmittroth

**BLACKBIRCH®
PRESS**

THOMSON

GALE

San Diego • Detroit • New York • San Francisco • Cleveland
New Haven, Conn. • Waterville, Maine • London • Munich

THOMSON

---*---

GALE

For more information, contact
The Gale Group, Inc.
27500 Drake Rd.
Farmington Hills, MI 48331-3535
Or you can visit our Internet site at http://www.gale.com

Photo credits: Cover Courtesy of Northwestern University Library; cover © National Archives; cover © Photospin; cover © Perry Jasper Photography; cover © Picturequest; cover © Seattle Post-Intelligencer Collection, Museum of History & Industry; cover © PhotoDisc; cover © Library of Congress; pages 5, 11, 12 (bottom), 13 (bottom), 15–22, 25–27 © Marilyn "Angel" Wynn, nativestock.com; page 6 © Corel Corporation; pages 7-10 © North Wind Picture Archives; pages 12 (top), 13 (top) © Library of Congress; page 14 © AP Photo/David Zalubowski; page 23 © Denver Public Library Western History Collection, X-32370; page 30 (left) © Denver Public Library Western History Collection, X-32358; page 30 (right) © Denver Public Library Western History Collection, X-32373; page 29 © Mario Villafuerte/Getty Images

LIBRARY OF CONGRESS CATALOGING-IN-PUBLICATION DATA

Arapaho / Marla Felkins Ryan, book editor ; Linda Schmittroth, book editor.
    v. cm. — (Tribes of Native America)
Includes bibliographical references and index.
Contents: Name — History — Sand Creek massacre — Government — Current tribal issues.
  ISBN 1-56711-587-X (alk. paper)
  1. Arapaho Indians—History—Juvenile literature. 2. Arapaho Indians—Social life and customs—Juvenile literature. 3. Sand Creek Massacre, Colo., 1864—Juvenile literature. [1. Arapaho Indians. 2. Indians of North America—Great Plains.] I. Ryan, Marla Felkins. II. Schmittroth, Linda. III. Series.

  E99.A7A73 2004
  978.004'973—dc21

                                                          2003002625

Printed in United States
10 9 8 7 6 5 4 3 2 1

Table of Contents

ARAPAHO

Name

The name Arapaho comes from the Pawnee word
tirapihu, which means "trader." The name also comes
from the Kiowa's name for the tribe, Ahyato, and the
Crow word *alappaho*. The Arapaho call themselves
I*nuna-ina* or *Hinono'eno*. These names mean "our
people," "sky people," or "roaming people."

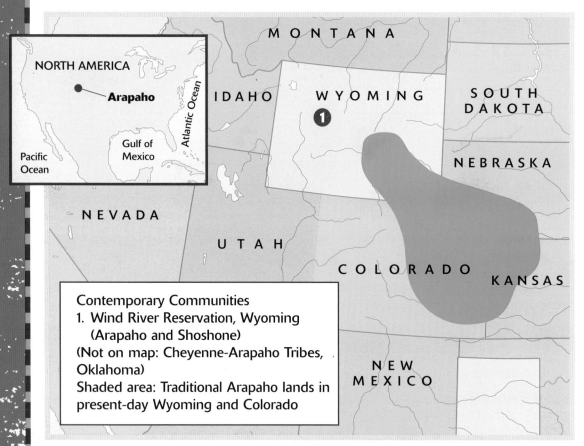

NORTH AMERICA

Arapaho

Atlantic Ocean

Pacific Ocean

Gulf of Mexico

MONTANA

IDAHO

WYOMING ❶

SOUTH DAKOTA

NEBRASKA

NEVADA

UTAH

COLORADO

KANSAS

NEW MEXICO

Contemporary Communities
1. Wind River Reservation, Wyoming
   (Arapaho and Shoshone)
(Not on map: Cheyenne-Arapaho Tribes,
Oklahoma)
Shaded area: Traditional Arapaho lands in
present-day Wyoming and Colorado

Arapaho on the Wind River Reservation in Wyoming play basketball during a powwow break.

Where are the traditional Arapaho lands?

In the 1700s, the Northern Arapaho lived in southern Wyoming and northern Colorado. The Southern Arapaho lived in western Oklahoma and southern Kansas. Today, the Northern Arapaho share the Wind River Reservation in Wyoming with the Shoshone tribe. The Southern Arapaho live on the Cheyenne-Arapaho Reservation in western Oklahoma.

The museum at the Wind River Reservation preserves artifacts from the Arapaho's rich history.

The Arapaho have lived near the Wind River Mountain Range (pictured) in Wyoming since the 1700s.

What has happened to the population?

Before the U.S. government set up Indian reservations, there were about 3,000 Arapaho. By 1861, only 750 Northern Arapaho and 1,500 Southern Arapaho were left. In a 1990 population count by the U.S. Bureau of the Census, 5,585 people said they were Arapaho. Another 1,319 people said they were Northern Arapaho, and 14 people said they were Southern Arapaho.

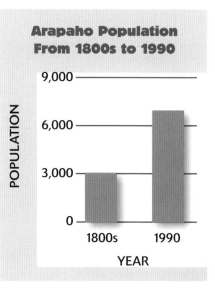

Arapaho Population From 1800s to 1990

POPULATION

9,000

6,000

3,000

0

1800s   1990

YEAR

Origins and group ties

The Arapaho first lived near the Great Lakes—perhaps in Minnesota or Canada. French explorers called one group of Arapaho the Gros Ventre (pronounced *grow VAHNT*). The reason for the name, which means "Big Belly," is unknown, but it has stuck.

In the mid-1660s, the Arapaho moved to the Great Plains. As they roamed the plains, they hunted buffalo on horseback. The Arapaho were peaceful. They let gold seekers and white settlers travel safely through Arapaho lands on their way west. Some white settlers decided to stay. They took over the Arapaho's hunting grounds. Cut off from their land, the tribe was not able to hunt buffalo. In the 1800s, the Arapaho split into two groups to hunt for the now scarce buffalo herds. Unable to find food, the Arapaho finally agreed to move onto reservations.

White settlement of Arapaho lands brought an end to the Arapaho's buffalo-hunting lifestyle.

HISTORY

• Timeline •

1600s to mid–1700s:
The Arapaho migrate from the Great Lakes region onto the Great Plains and become hunters

1607
English colonists settle Jamestown, Virginia

1835
The Arapaho divide into two groups. The Northern Arapaho settle near the North Platte River in Wyoming. The Southern Arapaho settle near the Arkansas River in Colorado.

1861
American Civil War begins

1864
At least 130 Southern Arapaho and Cheyenne—many of them women and children—are killed by U.S. Army troops during the Sand Creek Massacre

1865
Civil War ends

From Great Lakes to Great Plains

Around the year 1000 B.C., the Arapaho lived in the Great Lakes region. Over the years, they slowly moved south and west until they reached the Great Plains. On the plains, they gave up their farms and became hunters.

By the 1700s, the Arapaho lived in tepees. Their homes were covered with animal skins. They followed the great buffalo herds wherever they roamed. After Spanish explorers brought horses to the New World, the Arapaho were able to hunt on horseback.

After the Arapaho became a hunting people, they used easily transportable tepees for shelter.

The arrival of white settlers resulted in drastic changes to the Arapaho's way of life.

Relations with neighbors

The Arapaho traded goods with tribes that farmed. They traded meat and animal hides to the Hidatsa and Mandan tribes for beans, corn, and squash. At the same time, they led raids and fought against other tribes, often to get more horses.

In the mid-1800s, white newcomers began to invade Arapaho lands. Some white settlers wanted to make their homes there. Other groups were on their way to find gold in California. Their wagon trains upset the buffalo herds' need to roam freely. Often, scared buffalo ran in different directions and were lost from the herd. The Arapaho found it hard to find and hunt buffalo. Tribes had to fight each other for the small amount of game and land left on the plains.

The Arapaho began to trade with whites for guns and knives to fight their enemies. When non-Indians began to hunt on the plains, there was even less game for the tribes. The Arapaho began to depend on whites for food and clothing. Sometimes, they were paid in food and other

1867
The Southern Arapaho are placed on a reservation, which they share with the Cheyenne, in Oklahoma

1869
Transcontinental Railroad is completed

1878
The Northern Arapaho move onto the Wind River Reservation, which they share with the Shoshone, in Wyoming.

1917–1918
WWI fought in Europe

1941
Bombing at Pearl Harbor forces United States into WWII

1945
WWII ends

1950s
Reservations no longer controlled by federal government

1989–1990
The National Museum of the American Indian Act and the Native American Grave Protection and Reparations Act bring about the return of burial remains to native tribes

goods to escort wagon trains through the territory of tribes known to attack white settlers.

Division in the Arapaho tribe

Around 1835, the Arapaho split into two groups. One group was the Northern Arapaho. They moved near the Rocky Mountains in present-day Wyoming. The other group was the Southern Arapaho. They settled along the Arkansas River in present-day Colorado. The two groups still keep in close contact with one another.

The Arapaho were one of eleven tribes to sign the Fort Laramie Treaty of 1851. This agreement set aside large areas of land for the Indian tribes. Soon, white settlers wanted this land, too. The Arapaho were a peaceful tribe, but they took part in several battles to control the Great Plains.

The Arapaho and white settlers lived peacefully in and around Fort Laramie, Wyoming (pictured), until the whites' desire for Arapaho land led to conflicts.

Sand Creek Massacre

The conflict between Plains Indians and white settlers became deadly in November 1864. Cheyenne chief Black Kettle told the U.S. government that he wanted peace. He asked to be led to a safe place. The government sent the chief, his people, and members of the Arapaho tribe to Sand Creek in Colorado. The Indians lived peacefully there for a few weeks. Early one morning, that peace ended when American soldiers attacked the Indians as they slept. Almost 130 people were killed in the attack, which became known as the Sand Creek Massacre. Among the victims were Southern Arapaho leader Left Hand and many women and children. To fight back, the Southern Arapaho joined the Cheyenne in a war against the whites. The war lasted for six months.

This buffalo-hide painting shows Native Americans fleeing U.S. soldiers during the Sand Creek Massacre.

After the war

By 1867, many Southern Arapaho had died from illness or lack of food. Many more had been killed in the war. Tribal leaders finally agreed to live on a reservation. They gave up their homelands to live with a tribe of Cheyenne in western Oklahoma.

The Arapaho held meetings with other tribes to determine how they would share reservation lands.

This modern-day Arapaho dancer celebrates a culture preserved by his ancestors.

The Northern Arapaho resisted the government's demands to settle on a reservation. In 1878, they finally agreed to accept lands on the Wind River Reservation in Wyoming. They had to share the reservation with their former enemies, the Shoshone. After some tense times, the two tribes reached an agreement. They would live together but keep their own cultures and forms of government.

On the reservations, the Arapaho were encouraged to forget their traditional lifestyle. The U.S. government wanted the Indians to dress and act like whites. The Arapaho did not like this idea. They fought to keep their traditional ways of life. The Northern Arapaho were better able to resist the pressure to change their ways because Wyoming is the center of Arapaho religious life. Each year, the Southern Arapaho travel to the Wind River Reservation for powwows, rituals, and dances. Northern and Southern Arapaho come together to sing and dance at festivals.

This 1900 painting shows Arapaho gathered in a Ghost Dance. The Ghost Dance religion promised to restore the Arapaho's old way of life.

Religion

The Arapaho were very religious. They believed in a Creator who made the world and the Arapaho people. They prayed and offered gifts to the Creator. In return, they believed the Creator would give them health and happiness. Their most sacred object was the flat pipe. This pipe represented the power of the Creator on Earth.

The Sun Dance was an important ceremony in the Arapaho religion. It took place once a year. Before the dance, an Arapaho did not eat or sleep for many days. At the center of the Sun Dance was the Sacred Wheel. The wheel was decorated with pictures of the Sun, Earth, sky, wind, and water.

In the late 1800s, missionaries tried to convert the Arapaho to Christianity. Some Arapaho became Christians, but others joined the Ghost Dance religion. Founded by a Paiute Indian named Wovoka, the religion believed in a future time without white people. There would be plentiful game to hunt. Also, the dead ancestors of the Indians would return to life.

The flat pipe was the Arapaho's most sacred object.

Today, many Arapaho belong to the Native American Church. The church combines Christian and Native American beliefs and rituals. It has an all-night ceremony of chants, prayers, and meditation. Many Arapaho also take part in the Sweat Lodge ceremony. It is a special ritual that uses a sweat bath to clean a person's spirit.

Government

Arapaho men gained power within the tribe from the number of horses they captured in raids. If a man had many horses and was a noble person, he might be picked as leader of his group. Important decisions were made by all the adult men in the tribe and some older women. The opinions of leaders and elders were the most valued.

Today, a joint tribal government runs the Cheyenne-Arapaho Reservation in Oklahoma. Four members from each tribe are elected to serve four-year terms.

Arapaho leaders such as Robert Tabor (front) are elected to serve with heads of other tribes in a joint tribal government.

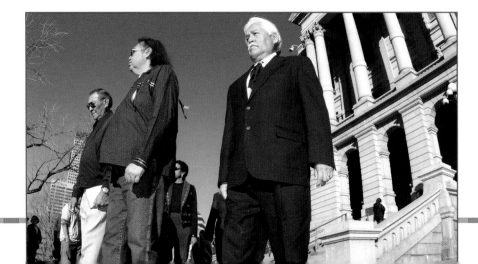

Economy

The Arapaho gave different chores to men and women. Even though men and women had different jobs, their work was equal in value. Long ago, the Arapaho were farmers. When they moved to the Great Plains, they hunted buffalo for meat. They used the buffalo's skin to make clothing or covers for their tepees. Because horses were needed to hunt buffalo, a man's wealth was measured in the number of horses he owned.

By the mid-1800s, the buffalo had nearly died out. Weakened by illnesses and a lack of food, tribe members sometimes stole farm animals from white settlers. When the U.S government began to donate food to the poor and hungry Arapaho, dishonest workers often cheated the Indians out of their share.

The Arapaho slowly began to support themselves. They ran farms and cattle ranches. They also sold reservation lands to whites. Today, some Northern and Southern Arapaho work in casinos, bingo parlors, and food stores to earn money. The Northern Arapaho raise prize cattle and horses. Most Southern Arapaho own little land and are very poor.

After the destruction of the buffalo herds, the Arapaho returned to farming, their way of life before moving to the Great Plains.

DAILY LIFE

Buildings

The Arapaho lived in tepees. These homes were easy to move as the tribe roamed the Great Plains to follow the buffalo herds. When the whole tribe came together to hunt, all the tepees were arranged in a large circle. Each family built its own tepee. Wooden poles were set into the ground in the shape of a cone. About fifteen to twenty buffalo hides were stretched over the top to cover the poles. After the buffalo grew scarce, tepees were covered with canvas.

Tepees provided effective, portable shelter for Arapaho families.

In the winter, the Arapaho moved to the foothills of the Rocky Mountains. In the mountains, they were

sheltered from the harsh weather. They camped in groups of twenty to eighty families. For extra warmth, dirt was piled in mounds around the outside of the tepees. The inside had a sleeping platform and a fire fueled with buffalo dung.

Food

Before the herds were nearly killed off the late 1800s, buffalo was the Arapaho's main food source. Men also hunted deer, elk, and smaller wild animals.

Berries, dried meat, and roots were part of the Native American diet.

The Arapaho would not eat bear. They believed that bears were their ancestors.

Arapaho women gathered roots and berries to eat fresh or to make into a soup. A favorite meal was a stew made of meat and potatoes or turnips. The Arapaho liked to drink a tea made with wild herbs.

Clothing

Most Arapaho clothing was made of deer or elk hides. Women used the skins to make long dresses, leggings, and moccasins. Arapaho men also wore shirts and breechcloths. These garments had front and back flaps that hung from the waist. In the

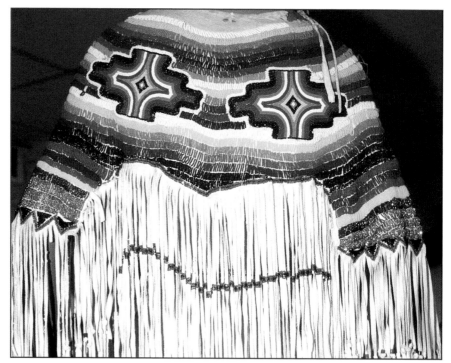

The intricate beadwork on a woman's deerskin dress shows the skill of its Arapaho maker.

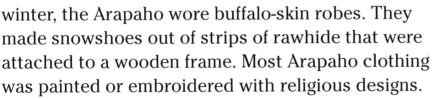

Moccasins such as these kept the Native Americans' feet warm and protected.

winter, the Arapaho wore buffalo-skin robes. They made snowshoes out of strips of rawhide that were attached to a wooden frame. Most Arapaho clothing was painted or embroidered with religious designs.

The Arapaho liked to decorate their bodies with tattoos. They pricked their skin with cactus needles and rubbed charcoal into the wounds. Men usually had three small circles across their chests. Women had a small circle on their foreheads.

Healing practices

The Arapaho believed that people could become sick if they thought or spoke of illness or death.

People could also become ill if they did not show proper respect to the Creator. When a person became sick, relatives would open the person's medicine bundle and pray. (The medicine bundle was a pouch with objects sacred to its owner.) Sometimes, people offered gifts of food, land, or even flesh to make their loved ones well again. In extreme cases, they would ask a medicine person called a shaman (pronounced SHAH-mun or SHAY-mun) for help.

Education

Arapaho children saw all adults as their mothers and fathers. To learn, they watched and imitated

Toys reflected the roles children would take in their adult lives.

adults. Respected elders were often invited to dine and tell stories of their life experiences.

Toys were smaller versions of adult items. These items helped to teach children their future adult roles. Girls played with tiny tepees and dolls. Dolls were not treated like babies because the Arapaho believed that even to mention a baby could cause pregnancy. Boys played war and hunting games.

After the Arapaho moved to the reservations, their children were sent away to boarding schools. Some boarding schools were set up on the reservations. Other schools were often great distances from home. Children were cut off from their parents. They were forbidden to use their native language. The Arapaho did not punish their children. But school workers often treated Arapaho children harshly.

Boarding schools treated Arapaho children harshly and forced them to conform to white standards.

On the Wind River Reservation, it is still the custom for elders to teach Arapaho children. Today, children have little contact with people outside the reservation until they graduate from reservation schools. Arapaho children in Oklahoma attend local public schools, colleges, and vocational-technical centers.

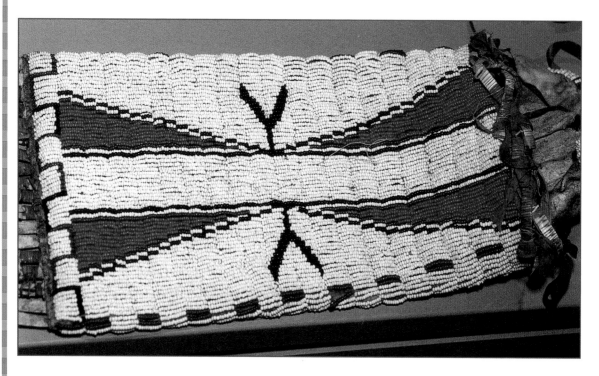

An Arapaho artist's dream inspired the design on this beaded bag.

Arts

Ideas for their artwork came to the Arapaho in dreams. Talented women artists painted these visions onto beautiful containers. They also used these designs in embroidery for medicine bundles and jewelry.

CUSTOMS

Childhood

The Arapaho believed that the four stages of life matched the four directions of the wind. These stages were childhood, youth, adulthood, and old age. Each stage had special rituals. As soon as a baby was born,

Young boys learned hunting skills as part of their growth into adulthood.

for example, older relatives marked the infant's face with red paint. They prayed for the baby to be strong and healthy. Between the ages of two and five, Arapaho children had their ears pierced. This ritual helped children learn to deal with future pain and hardship. As they approached puberty, boys and girls were separated from one another. As they began to prepare for adult life, boys joined special societies. Girls spent most of their time with the older women of the tribe. They dressed modestly and learned about women's duties.

Societies

While still young boys, Arapaho males began to work through eight military societies. As boys became young men, they entered the Kit Fox Lodge. After they gained a certain level of skill and bravery, they would move on to the next society. These societies had names like the Tomahawk, Spear, or Dog Lodge. Graduation from each society brought more honor and new duties.

Seven tribal elders were part of a group called the Water-Pouring Old Men. They were the most respected members of the tribe. They led ceremonies and took care of the sacred flat pipe. They also prayed for the good health of the Arapaho people.

When the great herds of buffalo roamed the plains, Arapaho women had their own society. It was called the Buffalo Lodge. Members performed ceremonial dances for a successful hunt. They wore costumes and painted their faces white to look like buffalo. They blew on special whistles to attract the buffalo.

This tepee painting shows a buffalo hunter on horseback ready to spear his prey.

Hunting rituals

In the buffalo hunt, Arapaho men worked together on horseback. They chased down individual animals and cut them off from the rest of the herd. At first, they used bows and arrows to hunt buffalo. The bows were made of cedar wood and sinew. Later, Arapaho hunters used guns. They butchered the buffalo out on the prairie. They used flint or bone knives to carve up the animal. After they finished, the buffalo was brought back to the camp. Arapaho women smoked or dried the buffalo meat for

The Arapaho used bows and arrows to hunt buffalo. Guns later replaced these traditional weapons.

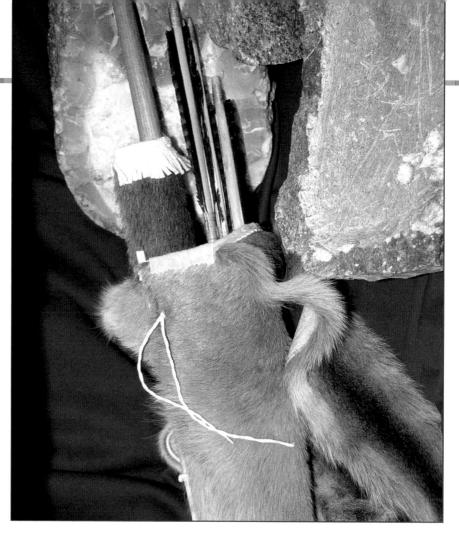

food. They used the skins to make clothing, tepee covers, or containers for water and food.

Marriage

An Arapaho woman's male relatives planned her marriage. She had the right to refuse their choice, but few women did so. On the wedding day, the families of the bride and groom exchanged gifts. Then, the bride's family hosted a feast. At this meal, the couple was allowed to sit together for the first time. After the wedding, the bride avoided contact with her husband's parents. To be equal, the groom also avoided contact with his new wife's parents.

Medicine bundles

Each member of the Arapaho tribe owned a medicine bundle. It held sacred objects that showed the person's relationship with the Creator. Arapaho

Every Arapaho carried a medicine bag like this one as a link to the Creator.

people had special visions that told them what to put in their medicine bundles. During times of illness or war, the Arapaho could use their medicine bundles to ask the Creator for help.

Current tribal issues

The Arapaho have faced many conflicts over land and water rights. In 1989, the U.S. Forest Service wanted to turn a sacred tribal site in Big Horn National Forest into a tourist attraction. The Arapaho tribe was able to stop this plan. Many other challenges faced the Arapaho in the 1990s. They worked to regain their native language and cultural traditions. The Arapaho also worked to find good wages and steady jobs.

Notable people

Black Spot (born c. 1824) was a daring warrior and Arapaho chief. He learned white American customs as a child. Accidentally left behind when his family moved camp in 1831, he was found by a white fur trapper. The trapper adopted the boy and renamed him Friday. The child went to school in St. Louis, Missouri. On a trip west in 1838, Black Spot was recognized by his Indian relatives. They brought him back into the Arapaho tribe. Because of his knowledge of white culture, Black Spot worked as an interpreter for treaty negotiations. He helped the whites and Indians to understand each other better when they made treaties. He was part of the group that gained the Wind River Reservation for the Arapaho people.

Modern-day Arapaho, like this crew of Native American firefighters, work together as they face a variety of contemporary issues.

Many Arapaho leaders helped Black Spot in negotiations with white people. Black Bear was one of these leaders. He was murdered by a group of white settlers in 1871. Medicine Man, who died around the same time, was also a revered healer. Black Coal took over for Medicine Man. He and Sharp Nose continued the work that allowed the Northern Arapaho to live in Wyoming.

Sharp Nose (left) and Black Coal (right) continued the work of Black Spot and Medicine Man, which enabled the Arapaho to keep reservation lands.

For more information

Arapaho Literature: www.indians.org/welker/arapaho.htm

Delaney, Ted. "Confronting Hopelessness at Wind River Reservation," *Utne Reader*, January/February 1990, pp. 61–63; excerpted from *Northern Lights*, October 1988.

Fowler, Loretta. *The Arapaho*. New York: Chelsea House, 1989.

Greymorning, Stephen. "Arapaho," in *Native America in the Twentieth Century: An Encyclopedia.* Mary B. Davis, ed. New York: Garland Publishing, 1994.

The Story of the Origin of the Arapaho People. Stories told by Pius Moss, an elder of the Arapaho Tribe on the Wind River Reservation. www.wyomingcompanion.com/wcwrr.html#arapaho

Glossary

Ghost Dance a religion that promised Native Americans a return to their old way of life

Powwow a Native American gathering or ceremony

Reservation land set aside for Native Americans by the government

Shaman a Native American priest who used magic to heal people and see the future

Tepee a tent used as a home by Native Americans

Treaty an agreement between two or more parties

Index